AaBbCcDdEeFfGgHh

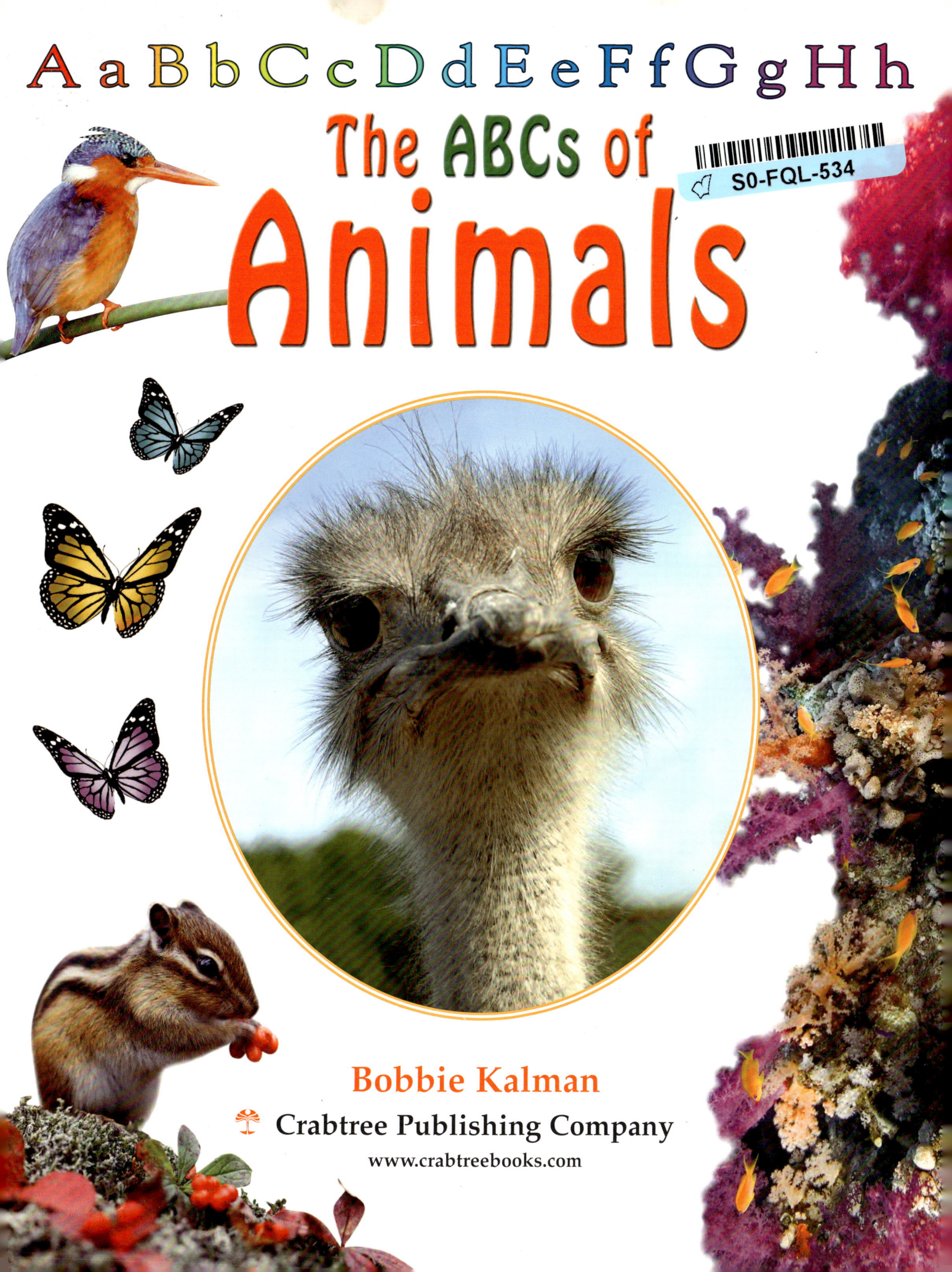

The ABCs of Animals

Bobbie Kalman

Crabtree Publishing Company
www.crabtreebooks.com

The ABCs of the Natural World

Created by Bobbie Kalman

Dedicated by Katherine Kantor
To my fiancé Matt–my best friend and the love of my life.
Thank you for all your love, kindness and support. You are the best!

Author and Editor-in-Chief
Bobbie Kalman

Editors
Reagan Miller
Robin Johnson

Photo research
Crystal Sikkens

Design
Bobbie Kalman
Katherine Berti
Samantha Crabtree (cover)

Production coordinator
Katherine Berti

Illustrations
Barbara Bedell: pages 4 (gorilla), 5 (mudpuppy),
　6 (toucan), 7, 11 (shark), 16, 17, 20, 22, 24, 25, 28
Anne Giffard: page 23
Katherine Berti: pages 4 (chimpanzee),
　11 (fish skeleton and elephant fish)
Bonna Rouse: pages 5 (all except mudpuppy),
　6 (avocet), 11 (eel)
Margaret Amy Salter: page 15
Tiffany Wybouw: page 26

Photographs
© BigStockPhoto.com: pages 21 (bottom), 22, 23 (bottom)
Marc Crabtree: page 9 (top)
© Dreamstime.com: page 28
iStockphoto.com: pages 5 (top right), 10 (right),
　25 (bottom), 26, 27, 30
© Shutterstock.com: front cover, back cover, pages 1 (all except bird),
　3, 5 (bottom left), 6, 7 (except insect), 8, 9 (bottom), 10 (left), 11, 12,
　14 (bottom), 15, 16, 17, 18, 19, 20, 21 (top), 23 (top), 25 (top), 29, 31
Other images by Adobe Image Library, Brand X Pictures, Creatas,
　Digital Stock, Digital Vision, and Photodisc

Library and Archives Canada Cataloguing in Publication

Kalman, Bobbie, 1947-
　　The ABCs of animals / Bobbie Kalman.

(The ABCs of the natural world)
Includes index.
ISBN 978-0-7787-3410-9 (bound)
ISBN 978-0-7787-3430-7 (pbk.)

　　1. Animals--Juvenile literature.　2. English language--Alphabet--Juvenile
literature.　I. Title. II. Series: ABCs of the natural world

QL49.K328 2007　　　　　j590　　　　　C2007-904241-4

Library of Congress Cataloging-in-Publication Data

Kalman, Bobbie.
　The ABCs of animals / Bobbie Kalman.
　　　p. cm. -- (The ABCs of the natural world)
　Includes index.
　ISBN-13: 978-0-7787-3410-9 (rlb)
　ISBN-10: 0-7787-3410-2 (rlb)
　ISBN-13: 978-0-7787-3430-7 (pb)
　ISBN-10: 0-7787-3430-7 (pb)
　1. Animals--Juvenile literature. 2. English language--Alphabet--
Juvenile literature.　I. Title. II. Series.

QL49.K2915 2007
590--dc22

2007026974

Crabtree Publishing Company

www.crabtreebooks.com　　　1-800-387-7650

Printed in the USA/102011/CG20110916

Copyright © 2008 CRABTREE PUBLISHING COMPANY. All rights reserved. No part of this publication may be reproduced, stored in a retrieval system or be transmitted in any form or by any means, electronic, mechanical, photocopying, recording, or otherwise, without the prior written permission of Crabtree Publishing Company. In Canada: We acknowledge the financial support of the Government of Canada through the Canada Book Fund for our publishing activities.

Published in Canada
Crabtree Publishing
616 Welland Ave.
St. Catharines, ON
L2M 5V6

Published in the United States
Crabtree Publishing
PMB 59051
350 Fifth Avenue, 59th Floor
New York, New York 10118

Published in the United Kingdom
Crabtree Publishing
Maritime House
Basin Road North, Hove
BN41 1WR

Published in Australia
Crabtree Publishing
3 Charles Street
Coburg North
VIC, 3058

Contents

Amazing animals	4
Beautiful birds	6
Cats are carnivores	8
Dingoes are wild dogs	9
Elephants or not?	10
Funny fish?	11
Gigantic giraffes	12
Habitats and homes	13
Insects and other... Invertebrates	14
Joeys are babies	16
Kangaroo and koala	17
Lots of lizards	18
Mammal mothers	19
Numbats, opossums, possums and quolls	20
Reptiles	22
Snakes and Tuataras	23
Ungulates	24
Vicunas	25
Wonderful whales	26
Xenarthrans	28
Yak about yaks	30
Zebra "ztripes"	31
Glossary and Index	32

AaAaAaAaAaAaAaAaAa

Amazing animals

There are many kinds of animals whose names start with the letter A. Ape starts with A. There are different kinds of apes. The ape below is an orangutan. Two other apes are chimpanzees and gorillas. Both chimpanzees and gorillas spend time in trees as well as on the ground. Orangutans spend almost all their time in trees.

chimpanzee   *gorilla*

A a A a A a A a A a A a A a A a A a A a

About amphibians

Amphibian also starts with the letter A. Amphibian means "two lives." Frogs are amphibians. They start their lives in water as eggs. The eggs hatch into **tadpoles**. Tadpoles breathe under water. Adult frogs can live on land and in water. They breathe above water.

Frogs and toads are **anurans**. Anurans are adult amphibians with no tails.

Amphibians with tails are mudpuppies, salamanders, newts, and sirens.

mudpuppy

salamander

newt

siren

B b B b B b B b B b B b B b B b

Beautiful birds

A bird is an animal with a beak, wings, and feathers. There are many kinds of birds. Some birds live in trees. Toucans live in trees. Some birds live near water. Avocets find food in water. Some birds even live on ice and snow. Which birds live on ice and snow?

toucan

avocet

Why do you think these birds are called lovebirds?

B b B b B b B b B b B b B b

Birds that do not fly

Some birds fly, but others do not. Penguins do not fly. Some penguins live in Antarctica, where it is very cold. Penguins use their wings to swim in the cold ocean waters.

CcCcCcCcCcCcCcCcCcCc

Cats are carnivores

Lions use their sharp teeth to bite the animals they hunt.

All cats are **carnivores**. Carnivores are animals that eat other animals. Wild cats are also **predators**. Predators hunt the animals they eat. The animals they hunt are called **prey**. Cats have sharp teeth that break the skin of their prey. Their rough tongues also help them eat the meat of animals.

Cheetahs are wild cats. They are the fastest animals on land. Their speed helps them catch prey.

D d D d D d D d D d D d D d D d D d D d

Dingoes are wild dogs

There are dozens of different kinds of dogs. Like cats, dogs are carnivores. Some dogs are wild dogs. They do not live with people. Wolves, coyotes, and dingoes are wild dogs. The dog below is a dingo. Some dogs are pet dogs. Dalmatians are pet dogs whose name starts with D. Dalmatians are white with black spots. Do you have a dog? What kind of dog is it?

dalmatian

Dingoes are wild dogs that live in Australia.

Elephants or not?

Elephants are the world's biggest land animals. An elephant has a huge body, big ears, two tusks, and a long trunk. Elephants can lift heavy things with their trunks, such as logs. Other animals have been named after elephants, but they are not elephants. Elephant seals live in oceans. They have big snouts that remind people of the trunks of elephants.

Elephant seals have snouts that look like elephant trunks.

tusk

trunk

Funny fish?

Some fish look like fish, and other fish do not. Most fish are bony fish. Bony fish have **skeletons** made of hard bone. The skeletons of other fish are made of **cartilage**. Cartilage is softer than bone, and it bends. Your ears are made of cartilage.

Clownfish are not funny, but they are colorful, like clowns. They are bony fish.

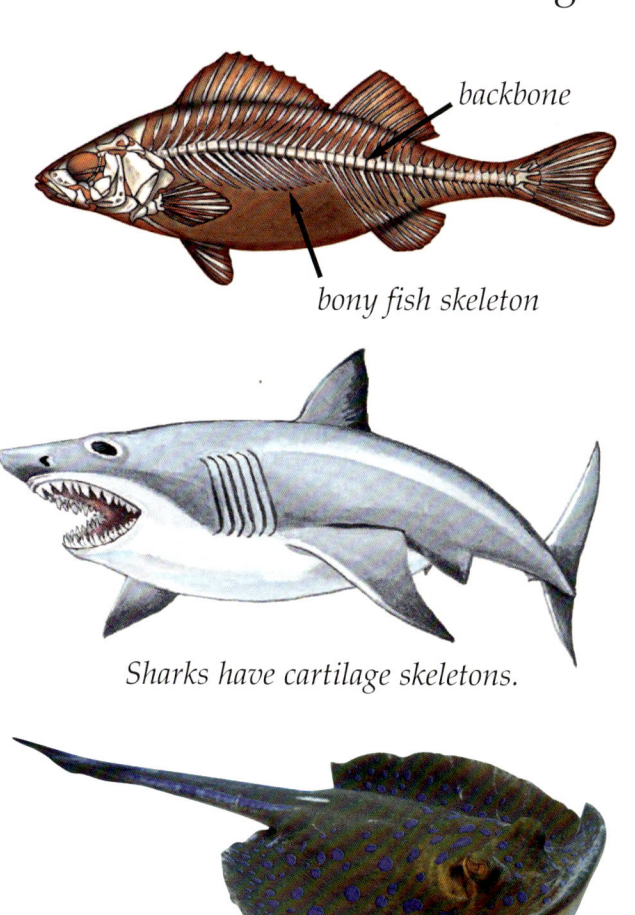

backbone

bony fish skeleton

Sharks have cartilage skeletons.

Eels are bony fish. They do not look like fish. They look more like snakes.

Rays also have cartilage skeletons.

Elephant fish have cartilage skeletons. Why do you think this fish is named after an elephant?

11

Gg Gg Gg Gg Gg Gg Gg Gg

Gigantic giraffes

Giraffes are gigantic! They have long necks. Long necks make giraffes very tall! Giraffes can eat leaves that are at the tops of trees. Giraffes live in **savannas**. Savannas are big grassy areas in hot, dry places. Savannas have long grasses and a few bushes and trees.

Hh Hh Hh Hh Hh Hh Hh Hh
Habitats and homes

The savanna is the giraffe's **habitat**. Habitats are the natural places where animals live. Some animals have homes in their habitats. For example, an owl's habitat is a forest, and its home is a hole in a tree. Foxes live in forest habitats, too, but their homes are not in trees. Their homes are hidden on the ground.

I i I i I i I i I i I i I i I i I i I i I i I i I i

Insects and other...

Insects are small animals. Insects have three body sections: the head, the thorax, and the abdomen. All adult insects have six legs. Insects also have two **antennae** on their heads. Antennae are feelers. Insect bodies have hard coverings called **exoskeletons**.

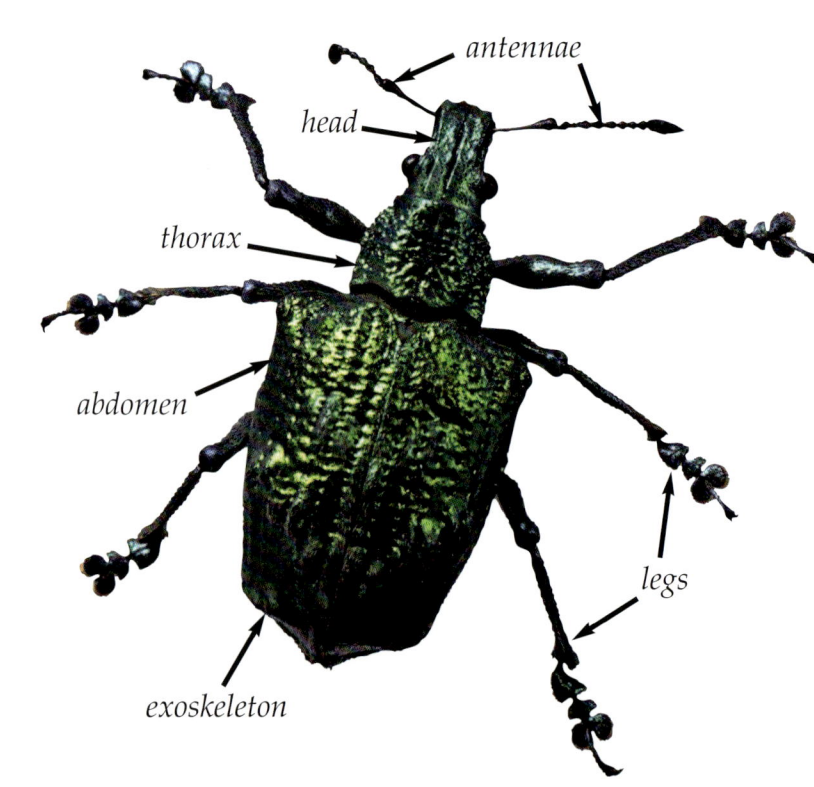

antennae
head
thorax
abdomen
exoskeleton
legs

Some insects have one or two pairs of wings. Dragonflies have two pairs of wings.

Invertebrates

Most of the animals on Earth are **invertebrates**. Invertebrates are animals that have no backbones or skeletons inside their bodies. Insects are invertebrates. Many other invertebrates live in oceans. Lobsters, clams, and nautiluses are invertebrates that live in oceans.

nautilus

lobster

clam

This sea star is an invertebrate.

An octopus is an invertebrate. It has a soft body and does not have a shell.

Many invertebrates have hard shells. All these seashells are the shells of invertebrates.

Joeys are babies

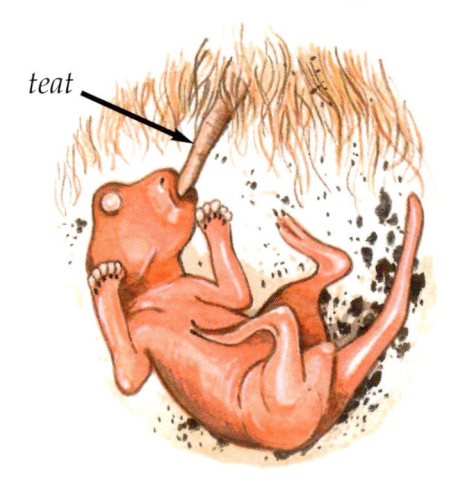

teat

*This kangaroo joey is drinking milk from a **teat** inside its mother's pouch.*

Joeys are baby kangaroos. Baby koalas are called joeys, too. Kangaroo and koala joeys live in their mothers' **pouches**, or pockets. They drink their mothers' milk and grow. When a joey gets bigger, it comes out of the pouch for a little while. The joey leaves the pouch when it can feed itself.

This kangaroo joey still drinks its mother's milk, but it is starting to eat adult food, too.

K k K k K k K k K k K k K k K k K k K k

Kangaroo and koala

A kangaroo's pouch is at the front of the kangaroo's body. A koala's pouch is near the koala's tail. Both kangaroos and koalas belong to a group of animals called **marsupials**. Meet more marsupials on pages 20-21.

Ll Ll Ll Ll Ll Ll Ll Ll Ll Ll Ll Ll Ll Ll

Lots of lizards

Lizards are animals with four legs, long bodies, and long tails. Lizards are **reptiles** (see page 22). Lizards can be small, like these three geckos. Lizards can also be huge! Komodo dragons are the largest lizards. Komodo dragons live in Indonesia on four small islands. One island is called Komodo Island.

*Komodo dragons live on land, but they are good swimmers. They swim from one island to another. They live in underground **burrows** to stay cool.*

M m M m M m M m M m M m
Mammal mothers

Mammals are a group of animals. Most mammals have hair or fur on their bodies. Pigs are mammals. Horses are mammals. People are mammals, too. Mammal mothers make milk in their bodies to feed their babies. They teach their babies how to look after themselves.

The baby horse on the right and the piglets below are drinking milk.

NnOoNnOoNnOoNnOoNnOo
Numbats, opossums,

Numbats live in Australia. They eat mainly termites.

Like kangaroos and koalas, numbats, opossums, possums, and quolls are marsupials. Marsupials are mammals. Most marsupial mothers have pouches. Their babies live in the pouches and drink milk. Numbats have no pouches. An opossum has a small pouch with many teats. Each baby hangs on to a teat to drink milk.

The Virginia opossum is the only opossum in North America. It is also the only marsupial in North America.

20

possums and quolls

Possums

Possums and opossums are not the same. They belong to different groups of marsupials, and they do not live in the same places. The animal on the right is a common brushtail possum. Her baby is riding on her back.

Quolls

A quoll mother has up to twenty babies, but she can only feed about ten. Quolls are carnivores. They hunt lizards, birds, frogs, and worms. They also eat garbage. Some people think quolls look like cats. What do you think?

R r R r R r R r R r R r R r R r R r R r R r R r R r
Reptiles

Crocodiles and alligators, turtles and tortoises, snakes and lizards, and tuataras are all reptiles. Most reptiles are carnivores. Alligators and crocodiles are big reptiles that can eat animals as large as deer.

Most reptiles hatch from eggs.

*Reptiles are **cold-blooded** animals. The bodies of cold-blooded animals are the same temperature as that of their surroundings. This alligator and turtle are warming their bodies in the sun.*

Ss Tt Ss Tt Ss Tt Ss Tt Ss Tt Ss Tt
Snakes and tuataras

Snakes are reptiles with long, thin bodies. They do not have legs. Most snakes move by **slithering** on the ground. To slither is to slide on the belly. Like all reptiles, snakes have skin made of **scales**. Scales protect a snake's body.

The reptile below is a tuatara. Tuataras have lived on Earth for millions of years—even before the dinosaurs lived here!

The green tree python above lives in trees. It wraps its long body around branches.

Tuataras are carnivores. They eat bird eggs, spiders, and insects.

U u U u U u U u U u U u U u U u U u

Ungulates

Ungulate means "animal with hooves." Horses and rhinos are ungulates. **Odd-toed ungulates** have hooves with one toe or three toes. **Even-toed ungulates** have hooves with two toes or four toes. Both horses and rhinos are odd-toed ungulates.

A horse's hoof has one toe.

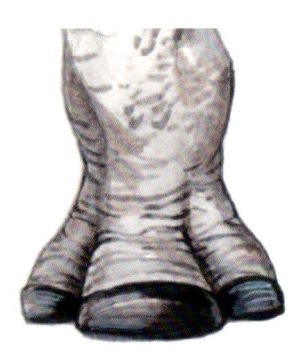

A rhino's hoof has three toes.

Vicunas

Vicunas are even-toed ungulates. They have two toes on their hooves. Vicunas belong to the camel family. The animal on the right is a camel. Camels live in the desert, but vicunas live high up on mountains in South America. Vicunas eat short grasses. Their sharp front teeth never stop growing.

A camel's hoof has two toes.

W w W w W w W w W w W w W w

Wonderful whales

Whales are mammals that live in oceans. Some whales have **baleen** in their mouths. Baleen is like a filter that catches tiny animals called **krill**. The humpback whale below takes a big gulp of water. It then pushes the water out of its mouth. The krill get stuck in the whale's baleen. This picture shows a whale's baleen.

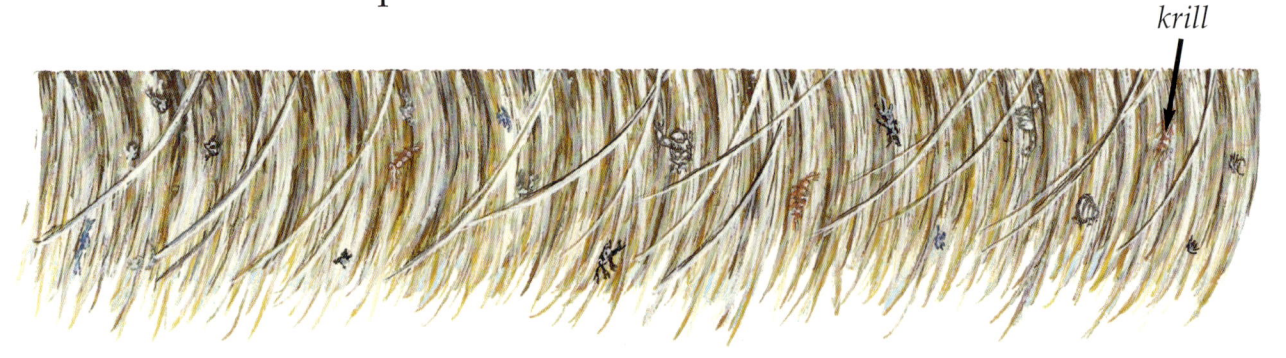

krill

baleen

Mammals must breathe air. They come to the surface of water to breathe.

W w W w W w W w W w W w W w

Whales with teeth

Toothed whales are smaller than baleen whales are. Dolphins are toothed whales. They use their many sharp teeth to catch prey. They swallow small prey whole. They tear bigger prey into pieces and then swallow the pieces.

Orcas are the biggest dolphins. They hunt fish, seals, and other dolphins. Orcas are also called "killer whales."

This dolphin has caught a fish with its sharp teeth. It will swallow the fish whole.

27

Xenarthrans

Xenarthran is a weird name for three very weird animals. They are anteaters, sloths, and armadillos. Xenarthrans are mammals that live in North America and South America. They have few or no teeth, and they have very small brains. The xenarthran in this picture is a southern tamandua anteater. It lives in the rain forests of South America. This anteater spends most of its time in trees. It sticks out its long tongue and sucks up ants and termites.

armadillo

X x X x X x X x X x X x X x X x X x X x X x X x X x

Hang on slothy, hang on!

This two-toed sloth and its baby are hanging upside down from a tree branch. Sloths sleep and eat while hanging. They sleep from 15 to 18 hours a day! They move very slowly. Sloths eat mainly tree leaves, but they also eat insects and small lizards. Sloths come down from the trees once a week to get rid of waste from their bodies.

Yak about yaks

Yaks, cows, and buffalo belong to the same animal family. People raise yaks for their milk and meat. They also use yaks to carry loads. Both male and female yaks have horns. Some yaks live in a place called Tibet, high up on the Himalaya Mountains. You can see the mountains in the picture. They are so high, that they are above the clouds.

ZzZzZzZzZzZzZzZzZzZzZzZzZz

Zebra "ztripes"

Zebras belong to the horse family. They are wild horses with stripes. No one knows why zebras have stripes. People once thought that the stripes helped hide zebras from lions and other predators. Other people said the stripes helped keep insects away. Maybe zebras tell each other apart by their stripes. Why do you think zebras have stripes?

Glossary

Note: Some boldfaced words are defined where they appear in the book.
burrow A hole or tunnel dug by a small animal, in which it lives
cartilage Soft, bendable bonelike tissue found in the bodies of some fish
cold-blooded Having a body temperature that changes with an animal's surroundings
exoskeleton A hard body covering found on some animals such as insects and crabs
insect A small animal with six legs
mammal An animal that breathes air and drinks its mother's milk as a baby and which has hair or fur and a backbone
marsupial A mammal whose young lives in a pouch after it is born, where it drinks its mother's milk
reptile An animal with a backbone, cold blood, and scaly skin
scales Small bony parts that protect the skin of fish and reptiles
skeleton A frame of bones inside an animal's body
ungulate A mammal that has hooves

Index

amphibians 5
apes 4
babies 16, 19, 20, 21, 29
birds 6-7, 21, 23
bodies 10, 14, 15, 17, 18, 19, 23, 29
breathing 5, 26
carnivores 8, 9, 21, 22, 23
cartilage 11
eggs 5, 22, 23
elephants 10, 11
fish 11, 27
flying 7
food 6, 16
habitats 13
hooves 24, 25
hunting 8, 21, 27
insects 14, 15, 23, 29, 31
invertebrates 15
kangaroos 16, 17, 20
koalas 16, 17, 20
legs 14, 18, 23
lizards 18, 21, 22, 29
mammals 19, 20, 26, 28
marsupials 17, 20, 21
oceans 7, 10, 15, 26
people 9, 10, 19, 21, 30, 31
predators 8, 31
prey 8, 27
reptiles 18, 22, 23
savannas 12, 13
skeletons 11, 15
swimming 7, 18
tails 5, 17, 18
teeth 8, 25, 27, 28
ungulates 24, 25
water 5, 6, 7, 26
whales 26-27
wings 6, 7, 14

32